Books should be returned or renewed by the last
date above. Renew by phone **03000 41 31 31** or
online *www.kent.gov.uk/libs*

The Lost Kitten

Lucy Daniels

With special thanks to Tabitha Jones

For Ruby and Lily Cowley

Ilustrations by Jo Anne Davies for Artful Doodlers

ORCHARD BOOKS

First published in Great Britain in 2019 by The Watts Publishing Group

1 3 5 7 9 10 8 6 4 2

A CIP catalogue record for this book
is available from the British Library.

ISBN 978 1 40835 921 1

Printed and bound in Great Britain by Clays Ltd, Elcograf S.p.A

The paper and board used in this book are made from wood from responsible sources.

Orchard Books
An imprint of
Hachette Children's Group
Part of The Watts Publishing Group Limited
Carmelite House
50 Victoria Embankment
London EC4Y 0DZ

An Hachette UK Company
www.hachette.co.uk
www.hachettechildrens.co.uk

CONTENTS

CHAPTER ONE

"That must be it!" Amelia said. The grassy path that she and Sam were following disappeared into a tangle of bushes ahead, and she quickened her pace. "Gran said the wilderness is full of animals. I can't wait to see it!"

Suddenly, Sam's Westie puppy, Mac,

 let out an excited yip and strained at his leash. A fluffy white kitten sat washing its paws in the shadow of a bramble bush.

"Leave it!" Sam told Mac.

Amelia smiled as Mac planted his bottom and waited, looking up at Sam expectantly. *His training is really coming along!* she thought proudly.

The kitten didn't seem to notice Mac at all. Amelia kneeled and held her hand towards it. "Hello, you," she said. The little cat looked up at her with wide blue eyes. "Awww! You are so cute!" Amelia said. The kitten stretched up on its back legs and butted its head into her fingers. Then it let out a loud *MIAOOOW!*

Mac whimpered.

"It's just a kitten, Mac," Sam said, grinning. "You can't be scared!" But Mac scrabbled behind Sam, eyeing the kitten warily.

Amelia scratched the kitten behind the ears and it started to purr, almost as loudly as when Amelia's dad snored. She couldn't help giggling.

Sam led his puppy

towards the thicket, giving the kitten a
wide berth. "Let's explore!" he said.

Amelia felt a pang as she left the kitten
behind. But when she glanced back she
saw it happily batting at a fly, its saucer-
like blue eyes darting in all directions.
She followed Sam, pushing through
twisted branches.

They soon broke out into an area of
open, sunlit scrubland. A few tall, knobbly
oaks emerged from the undergrowth,
but most of the trees were saplings.
Wildflowers and long grass smothered
the ground, and insects and feathery
seeds filled the air, making everything
look hazy and golden.

Sam unclipped the lead from Mac's collar. "Off you go!" The puppy tore away, hurtling through the long grass with his ears back and his tail stuck out behind him.

"This place is amazing!" Amelia said, taking it all in. Then she frowned. "Or it *would* be, if there wasn't so much rubbish." She could see at least half a dozen drinks cans on the ground, along with crisp

packets, plastic bottles and even a dirty
old sock.

A buzz coming from near Amelia's feet
made her look down, just in time to see a
bee zip out from a small hole in the sun-
baked earth. "Look! A bumblebee nest!"
she said, pointing. But her excitement
changed to dismay as the bee buzzed
straight towards one of the empty drink
cans. Amelia quickly turned the can over,
so the bee couldn't get stuck inside. "This
place is such a mess!"

"You're right," Sam said, watching his
puppy dive out of sight between two
huge bushes. "I hope Mac doesn't eat
anything he shouldn't. We'd better keep

an eye on him." Sam pushed his way through the branches after his little dog. Amelia followed close behind, stomping down on brambles that snagged at her socks.

"Whoa!" Sam said. "Look at this!"

Mac was sniffing at the wall of a small rectangular building, smothered in ivy. The top part was covered with wooden slats with peeling white paint and it had a peaked roof that made Amelia think of gingerbread houses. *It must have been nice once*, she thought. But now branches poked up through the roof tiles and graffiti covered the brickwork.

Amelia peered in through the dark,

gaping window hole. Part of the roof had
fallen in, and weeds grew up through the
rubble.

"What is this place?" Sam asked.

"I don't know," Amelia said. "But it's
kind of spooky."

"Hello!" a deep male voice boomed
from behind them. Amelia and Sam
whirled around. It was Mr Banks. He
and his daughter Tiffany, their classmate,

were walking down the wide grassy path
that ran in front of the building. Trotting
ahead of them on a short lead came
Sparkle, Tiffany's little curly-haired white
dog. Tiffany munched on a chocolate
bar, ignoring her classmates.

"Hi there!" called Sam.

Amelia dropped to one knee to pet
Sparkle, just as Mac bounded up to say
hello. Tiffany rolled her eyes as the two
dogs circled each other, sniffing.

"So, you've found the old signal box!"
Mr Banks said. He pointed to a sign
sticking up from a ledge of crumbling
concrete. It was green with moss, but
Amelia could just make out the words

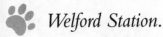

Welford Station.

"I didn't know there was a railway station in Welford!" said Amelia.

"Oh, it shut years before you were born," Mr Banks said, smiling. "Now all that's left is this footpath where the track used to be." He went to look more closely at the station sign.

"It's a total dump if you ask me," Tiffany muttered, tossing her chocolate wrapper on to the ground.

"Well, you don't need to make it worse!" Amelia said, picking up the wrapper and holding it out to her classmate.

Tiffany let out a sigh but took the

wrapper and shoved it in her pocket.
Then she suddenly frowned and tugged
at Sparkle's lead. "Leave it!" she said
firmly.

Sparkle stood completely still, half a
grubby doughnut clamped in his muzzle.
His black-button eyes were fixed on
Tiffany. He gave
his tail a hopeful
wag but Tiffany
didn't move a
muscle.

Finally, Sparkle
set the grimy
doughnut on the
ground. Right

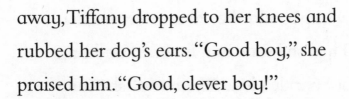

away, Tiffany dropped to her knees and rubbed her dog's ears. "Good boy," she praised him. "Good, clever boy!"

"That was amazing!" Amelia said. "The old Sparkle would never have obeyed you like that."

Tiffany got to her feet, smiling. "You were right about puppy classes," she said. "And I guess you're right about the rubbish, too. Who leaves half a doughnut, anyway?"

"Not me! That's for sure," Mr Banks said, walking back towards them. "Which reminds me, we need to get home for dinner."

The sunlight had started to fade. "We

should go too," Amelia told Sam.

After Sam had clipped the lead on
to Mac's collar, they all headed back
through the wilderness. Mr Banks
had parked in a layby beside the gate.
Tiffany lifted Sparkle into the boot,
then climbed into her seat. "See you at
school tomorrow!" she called to Sam and
Amelia.

But as Mr Banks got into the front seat,
Amelia noticed the little white kitten.
It was sitting right in the middle of the
road with its back to the car, cleaning its
paws. Amelia waved to Mr Banks and
pointed.

Mr Banks frowned at the kitten, then

honked his car horn. The sound was so loud that Amelia jumped, but the kitten kept right on washing.

"Here, kitty!" Sam called. Amelia made chirping sounds, but the kitten kept licking its paw.

Mr Banks shrugged theatrically, then started the engine. As soon as the car roared into life, the kitten leaped up, bristling all over, and scrambled away. *CRACK!* It smacked headfirst into the gate, let out a sickening screech and darted under the hedge.

Amelia's heart clenched. "Oh no!" she cried. "It's hurt!"

CHAPTER TWO

Amelia kneeled and put out her hand, trying to coax the kitten from its hiding place under the hedge. It yowled, and its fur stood on end. When Amelia tried reaching for it, the tiny creature hissed and spat.

"Is it all right?" Mr Banks asked,

crouching at Amelia's side. "I didn't mean to frighten it! I just wanted it to move." The kitten let out another strangled miaow.

"It hit its head pretty hard," Amelia said. "It sounds like it could be in pain."

"We should take it to Animal Ark," Sam said. "Does it have an ID tag?"

Amelia peered at the kitten, her cheek almost touching the ground. There was no tag on its collar. "No," she said. "We'll just have to take it in and worry about finding its owner later."

"I'll give you a lift," Mr Banks said. "It's the least I can do."

Amelia took off her school cardigan

24

and wrapped it over her hands, then reached under the hedge for the kitten. It let out a terrified screech and squirmed, but Amelia held the  animal firmly and drew it close to her chest. Surrounded by soft folds of fabric, the tiny kitten barely seemed to weigh anything at all.

Sam had already clambered into the back of Mr Banks's car with Mac curled at his feet. He leaned over to belt Amelia in as she was cradling the mewling kitten in her arms. Its pitiful cries tugged at her heart. Even Tiffany looked sorry as she glanced back over her shoulder from the front seat. Sparkle let out a growl from his carrier in the boot.

"Hush, Sparkle!" Tiffany said. "I hope the poor thing isn't badly hurt!"

The drive into Welford didn't take long, but once they reached town, Mr Banks got stuck in traffic. "Cars all over the place!" he said crossly. "We really need more parking spaces."

The tiny kitten didn't stop yowling the whole journey. By the time they reached Animal Ark, Amelia felt almost frantic with worry. *Please let the poor kitten be all right!*

26

Mr Banks stopped the car and Amelia scrambled out, keeping careful hold of the kitten. Sam thanked Mr Banks and hurried after her with Mac.

Inside Animal Ark, Amelia went straight to Julia at the reception desk, clutching her yowling bundle.

"What have we here?" Julia asked kindly.

"It bumped its head," Amelia said, unwrapping the kitten to show her. "It happened near the wilderness."

Julia's face brightened. "That's Tinkerbell," she said. "She belongs to the Girtz family. I should have known from her miaow – she's so noisy! Take a seat while I call Mrs Girtz. Mrs Hope will want to check her over."

Amelia sat down with Tinkerbell while Sam and Mac made friends with a black poodle wearing a head cone. Amelia stroked the kitten's fur, trying to keep her

calm despite all the strange noises and smells.

Before long, the door to the surgery swung open and Charlene Girtz hurried in, followed by her mother. Both looked worried, until Tinkerbell let out a yowl. Charlene grinned and made a beeline for the kitten.

Amelia smiled shyly. Charlene was in the year above her at school. Both her parents were professional artists, and Charlene was a talented painter, too – one of her pictures hung in the school hall. The Girtzes even looked arty. Mrs Girtz wore a black smock, smudged with paint, and Charlene had a streak of paint

on her forehead, below a wrap that held
back her curly hair.

"Poor Tink!" Charlene said, gently
lifting the noisy bundle from Amelia's
lap. "I was so worried when Julia called,
but it sounds like she's OK." Charlene
giggled. "She's by
far the noisiest of
our three kittens.
And that's saying
something!"

"Our cat Tiger
Lily recently gave
birth to a litter,"
explained Mrs
Girtz. "We've

named them Tinkerbell, Pan and Smee."

Amelia's heart leaped. "Sam and I can help you find homes for them! We rehomed a whole litter of stray kittens for Animal Ark."

"Oh, no!" Mrs Girtz said, smiling. "We're going to keep them all!"

Amelia blinked in surprise. Her kitten Star was a handful all by herself. *I can't imagine having* three *kittens,* she thought.

Just then, Mrs Hope called Tinkerbell in. Amelia led Charlene and her mother into the assessment room, leaving Sam to look after Mac. She and Sam always helped out when they were at Animal Ark – Mr and Mrs Hope had asked them to be official young helpers at the surgery.

"Hello, little one!" Mrs Hope said to the kitten. Then she smiled kindly at Charlene. "Pop Tinkerbell on the table, and I'll check her over."

Charlene unwrapped Tinkerbell from Amelia's cardigan and set her down. The kitten let out a long, high-pitched miaow, then kept right on mewing as Mrs Hope felt her all over and shone a

light into each of her blue eyes.

When she'd finished her checks, Mrs Hope frowned. "I can't see anything seriously wrong with her, but she does seem a little confused," she said. "I think it would be best if we kept her overnight, just to be on the safe side. How did the accident happen?"

"Sam and I found her near the old train station," Amelia said. "She got startled by a car and ran into a metal gate."

Mrs Hope sighed. "I'm glad nothing more serious happened. That place is in a terrible state. Some poor animal is bound to get tangled in plastic or eat

something poisonous." Mrs Hope turned to Charlene's mum. "Are you all right to come back tomorrow to fetch her? Hopefully she won't need any treatment. Just a good night's rest."

Mrs Girtz nodded. "We'd rather be safe than sorry! We'll come and get her after school."

As Mrs Hope took Tinkerbell through to the "hotel", where poorly animals stayed overnight, the kitten let out a loud, sad-sounding miaow. Charlene bit her lip as the door closed.

"Poor Tink!" Charlene said, still staring after her kitten. "She's never spent a night alone before. I wish I could stay to keep her company!" Mrs Girtz put an arm around her daughter's shoulders.

"She'll be all right," Mrs Girtz said.

Amelia nodded. "The hotel has plenty of blankets and toys. Mrs Hope will make sure Tinkerbell's comfy."

To Amelia's relief, Charlene smiled. "Thank you!" she said. "I just hope she's going to be all right!"

Amelia thought of the kitten's funny blue eyes and yowling voice. *I really hope so too!*

CHAPTER THREE

"Here's the last one," Sam said, pulling a rubber bone from a box and handing it to Amelia. She hooked it on to a display next to the others. They had helped unload a delivery of dog toys at Animal Ark after school.

Amelia heard the door to the surgery

swing open and turned to see Mrs Girtz come in with Charlene.

Julia looked up from the screen on her desk. "Hi, Charlene. Tinkerbell will be pleased to see you! I'll tell Mrs Hope you've arrived."

Spotting Sam and Amelia, Charlene tipped her head to one side quizzically. "Are you two *always* here?"

"We help out after school most days," Sam said proudly.

Mrs Hope poked her head around the door to the "hotel". "Come on in, all of you," she said. "Tinkerbell's doing really well."

Amelia and Sam followed Charlene

and her mum through the door. A pair of spaniels in crates wagged their tails as Mrs Hope led everyone towards a smaller, raised cage where Tinkerbell lay curled on a blanket.

"Why don't you get her out?" Mrs Hope said to Charlene.

Charlene unhooked the latch for the door. "Hello, Tink!" she said. She reached in to pick Tinkerbell up. As soon as her hand touched the kitten, Tinkerbell flinched and let out a startled squeak.

"Sorry, Tink!" Charlene said, nestling the white kitten against her jumper and

stroking her tufty ears. "She's always been a bit jumpy."

Amelia frowned. *She didn't seem jumpy in front of Mr Banks's car – not until he started the engine!*

"Pop her on the floor, so I can check how she's moving," Mrs Hope said.

Charlene set her kitten down on the tiles. After giving a big yawn that showed her pink tongue, Tinkerbell started to clean the fur on her neck, purring loudly to herself.

"Come on, Tink!" Charlene said. She made some kissing noises, but Tink didn't even look up. Amelia took a bell on a stick from the counter and waved it

above the kitten's head, making it jingle.

Tinkerbell ignored the sound completely.

"Let me try," Charlene said. She kneeled in front of her kitten and waggled the stick. Right away, Tinkerbell's eyes fixed on it. She sprang towards the bell and started to bat it with her paws.

As she watched the kitten playing happily, something suddenly clicked in Amelia's mind. *Tinkerbell only reacts to things she can see!*

Amelia turned to

Mrs Hope. "Could Tinkerbell be deaf?" she asked. "Only, she didn't act like she heard the bell when it was above her. And yesterday, it seemed like she didn't hear Mr Banks's car horn. She only moved when he started the engine."

Mrs Hope frowned thoughtfully. "It's certainly possible," she said. "Deafness is quite common in white cats with blue eyes. The engine probably made the whole car vibrate, and Tinkerbell must have felt it through the ground. That would also explain why she's so noisy – deaf cats can't hear how loudly they're miaowing."

Charlene's eyes were wide with worry.

"Is there any way to find out for sure?" she asked.

"It's fairly easy to test," Mrs Hope said. "You keep her attention, and I'll see if she can hear me behind her. Amelia – can you give Charlene a toy that doesn't make a noise?"

Amelia swapped the bell for a tuft of feathers on elastic. Charlene waved the feathers, and Tinkerbell's tail twitched as she followed them with her eyes. Then she hunkered down on all fours and pounced, snaring her prey. Tink chewed and clawed at the feathers happily, sending bits of coloured fluff flying.

While the kitten was busy, Mrs Hope

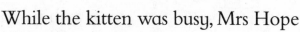

crept up behind her, and shouted
"TINK!"

Tinkerbell kept on playing.

Mrs Hope clapped her hands, but
Tinkerbell didn't react. Finally, the vet
took a whistle from a drawer and blew
it right behind the kitten. *Nothing!* The
spaniels in their cages both started to
bark, but Tinkerbell didn't seem to notice
a thing.

"It looks like you're right, Amelia," Mrs

Hope said. "Well done." Normally Amelia would be pleased to get praise from Mrs Hope, but watching the kitten playing  happily, unaware that anything was wrong, her chest tightened with worry. *What will happen to poor Tink now?*

Charlene put down the toy and scooped Tinkerbell into her arms, burying her face in the kitten's fur. "She really can't hear at all?" Charlene asked in a small voice.

"Don't worry," Mrs Girtz said, giving her daughter's shoulder a squeeze. "We will love her just the same."

"Tinkerbell can still lead a full life," Mrs Hope said. "But she'll need to be an indoor cat, for her own safety. Now that you know she's deaf, you can learn new ways to communicate with her."

"Like sign language?" Charlene asked, looking up.

"Exactly," Mrs Hope said. "Deaf cats can learn hand signs, and they can be trained to understand light signals too. You can even buy special light-up toys."

"You'll enjoy training her!" Mrs Girtz said, smiling at her daughter.

"I guess so," said Charlene sadly. She cradled Tinkerbell to her chest as if she never wanted to put her down. Amelia felt a rush of pity for the older girl, and suddenly had an idea.

"Sam and I trained Mac," she said. "If you like, we could help you train Tinkerbell?"

Charlene lifted her face from her kitten's fur. "That would be great," she said. "Could we get started tomorrow after school? You can meet Tinkerbell's brothers and stay for tea."

"Perfect!" Sam said, grinning.

"I'll do some research tonight," Amelia said. She reached out a hand and

scratched the fur on Tinkerbell's head.
The kitten lifted her pink nose and
nuzzled Amelia's fingers, then started
purring like an engine. Amelia smiled.
"This is going to be fun!"

CHAPTER FOUR

After school on Thursday, Amelia, Sam
and Charlene walked together to the
Girtzes' home. It was a converted barn
with shining solar panels on the roof,
down a country lane near the wilderness.
When they reached the front door,
Amelia smiled to see a pair of Egyptian-

style cat statues standing guard on either side. Even the brass knocker was in the shape of a cat's head.

"I'm home!" Charlene called, leading Sam and Amelia inside.

"Hi, darling!" her dad called from upstairs.

"Hello!" her mum called from the back of the house. "There are biscuits in the kitchen!"

Amelia and Sam followed Charlene into a big, open-plan living area with wooden beams criss-crossing the ceiling. The walls had been painted a rich purple but were mostly hidden by bookcases and paintings. Over the fireplace hung a

painting of a snow leopard, and a sphinx statue stood nearby. The more Amelia looked, the more carvings and pictures of cats she noticed.

"Wow!" Sam said. "You guys are crazy about cats, huh?"

"Pretty much," Charlene said. She picked up the biscuit tin on the way through the kitchen and led Sam and

Amelia into a conservatory. Half-finished
pictures propped on easels crowded the
space. The wicker chairs around the
edges of the room were piled high with
art materials.

"These are our cats," Charlene said,
standing before a painting of three

kittens curled
up around a
regal-looking
tortoiseshell.
Two of the
kittens were
tortoiseshell
too, and one
was totally

white. "That's Tiger Lily," Charlene said, pointing to the adult cat. "These are Pan and Smee. And of course you know Tinkerbell."

"Whoa – did you paint that?" Sam asked.

Charlene nodded. "It's not finished yet. I can't get Tinkerbell's nose quite right."

Amelia squinted at the delicate pink triangle Charlene had painted and couldn't see anything wrong with it. "It looks good to me!" she said. "You're an amazing artist!"

"Aww, thanks!" Charlene said, blushing a little. A sudden miaow made everyone turn to see Tiger Lily strut into the room, her tail held high. She was followed by three smaller, fluffy bundles – Smee, Pan and Tink. Tiger Lily trotted over to a cat flap in the door, nudged it with her nose and went out into the garden. Pan and Smee quickly followed her. But when Tink butted her nose against the flap, it stayed firmly shut.

Tinkerbell let out a long, loud miaow, stalking back and forth in front of the flap. Outside, Smee pounced on a leaf. Pan wiggled his little backside, then leapt on his brother, while Tiger Lily watched, delicately cleaning her paws.

"MIAOW!" Tink said again, looking up at Charlene with pleading blue eyes.

"Sorry, Tink," Charlene said,
grimacing. She turned to Amelia and
Sam. "The cat flap's been programmed
to recognise all the cats' microchips, but
we've taken Tink's out of the system so
she can't go out. She's pretty annoyed."

"And isn't she letting everyone know
all about it?" Mr Girtz said, grinning
as he came into the conservatory. "Ah!

There they are," he said, swooping on the biscuit tin and taking one. Just then, Tink started sharpening her claws on the leg of a wicker chair. "Oooh! No, you don't!" Mr Girtz said. He lifted the kitten gently in one hand, then set her down by a scratching post. Tink sidled away from it, her tail stuck up in the air.

"She never used to scratch the furniture," Charlene said sadly, once her dad had left. "She really hates being stuck indoors."

"Let's get her training started then,"
Amelia said. "It will take her mind off it."

"Good idea!" Charlene said. "What
should I do first?"

"I did some research on my tablet
last night," Amelia said. "One website
suggested to try stamping – the
vibrations should get her attention. And
if that works, you can pat the floor to get
her to come to you."

Charlene stomped on the floorboards.
Tink immediately turned her head, and
Amelia grinned. *It's working!* Charlene
knelt and patted the floor with one
hand. Tinkerbell's blue eyes widened. She
crouched, her ears pricked, then pounced.

"Ouch!"
Charlene
carefully
unhooked
the kitten's
tiny claws

from her hand. As she rubbed at the
scratches, Tink's blue eyes followed every
movement. Suddenly, she pounced again.
Charlene snatched her hand away before
the kitten could catch it.

"I think she finds hand signals a bit too
exciting," Sam said.

Amelia suddenly had an idea. "I
know," she said. "Why don't you try
purring? Another website said deaf cats

58

find that calming – they can feel the rumbles through your body."

"OK ..." Charlene said doubtfully. She picked Tinkerbell up and took a seat, holding the kitten still. Tink's fluffy tail twitched.

Charlene leaned over her kitten and started to purr. Her first attempt sounded more like a raspberry, and Amelia and Sam giggled. Tink stiffened, flicking back her ears. Eventually Charlene managed to produce a low, snoring sound in the back of her throat that wasn't too far off a purr. Even so, Tinkerbell squirmed in her hands, scrabbling to escape.

With a sigh, Charlene let the kitten

go. Tinkerbell shot across the room, her fur standing on end. Then she skittered sideways as if something had spooked her, spun around, and set about chasing her tail.

"She's got too much energy to learn anything right now!" Charlene said.

Amelia watched as the kitten flopped over on her side and started gnawing at the tip of her tail. "You might be right," she said.

"Kids! Time to eat!" Mrs Girtz called. With another sigh, Charlene led the way back through to the living area. Mr and Mrs Girtz were already seated at a table set with pasta, salad and garlic bread. Amelia's tummy rumbled. But before she and Sam could take their seats, a hideous tearing sound came from the conservatory.

"That'll be Tinkerbell making trouble again!" Mr Girtz said.

Charlene darted out of the room.
Amelia and Sam followed her back
into the conservatory. Amelia gaped in
dismay. Tink was clinging to Charlene's
painting, ripping it to shreds with her
claws!

"Your painting!" Sam cried.

Charlene looked pale. But somehow,
she managed to laugh. "Oh, Tink!" she
said. "I guess you didn't think much of
the nose I gave you either." She lifted the
kitten gently from the ruined picture and
gave her a quick squeeze before setting
her down. "And it looks like you *really*
don't like being a house cat. What are we
going to do with you?"

Hmm, Amelia thought, watching the kitten pad away. *There must be some way to make Tinkerbell happy at home. And I won't give up until I find it!*

63

CHAPTER FIVE

Excitement bubbled in Amelia's chest as she and Sam reached the Girtzes' house on Friday after school. "This is the perfect solution for a bored house cat!" Amelia said, as Sam rapped on the door. She was clutching a red kitten harness she'd picked up at Animal Ark.

Charlene looked so worried and pale as she opened the door that Amelia's excitement turned to alarm.

"Is everything all right?" Sam asked.

"Not really," Charlene said, as she led them inside. "Tink made a mess on my bedroom carpet while I was at school instead of using her litter tray."

"Ew!" said Sam, wrinkling his nose.

"Oh no!" Amelia held up the harness. "I've brought something that might help Tink. We can take her for a walk!"

Charlene frowned. "Really?" she asked. "I didn't know cat harnesses were a thing." Then she smiled and shrugged. "I guess it's worth a try. I'll get Tink –

she's sulking under my bed." Charlene
disappeared upstairs and came back
holding Tink, then took a seat with the
kitten on her lap.

"This bit goes over her head," Amelia
said, showing
Charlene the
padded collar.
"The rest goes
around her belly,
and clips together
at the side."

As Charlene
slipped the collar
on, Tinkerbell
squirmed and

hissed. "Come on, Tink!" Charlene coaxed, but the kitten twisted around and swiped Charlene's hand with her claws. "Ouch!"

"Let me help." Amelia held the kitten firmly with both hands, while Charlene put the harness around Tink's belly. Finally, Charlene fastened the clip and set Tinkerbell on the floor.

The kitten started walking backwards, her head writhing from side to side and her blue eyes rolling about wildly. When that didn't get rid of the harness, Tink clawed at the lead, then flopped over and started to chew it. Eventually she gave up and sat hunched, her fur bristling, and

her eyes half-closed in disgust.

Charlene picked up the end of the lead
and gave it a gentle tug. The kitten's
head whipped around, and she let out a
yowl. Charlene pulled again. Tink stood
up and staggered a few steps, before
flopping over again.

"Maybe she'll forget about the harness
when she's outside," Sam said. "We
should take her on a proper walk."

"Good idea," Amelia said. "We can bring some cat treats to coax her along."

Grabbing a bag of treats from the kitchen, Charlene led Amelia and Sam to the path outside their house. She set Tink

on the grass. The kitten swiped at her lead, but Amelia held a fish-shaped treat close to the kitten's face. As Tink looked up, her nose twitching, Amelia pulled the treat away, holding it just out of reach. Tinkerbell let out a miaow, then swaggered towards the treat. Amelia let her snaffle it up as a reward. Then she moved slightly further away and held out another treat. Slowly, and with plenty of noisy yowling from the kitten, Amelia, Charlene and Sam managed to get Tink almost as far as the wilderness.

"Have you seen the old signal box?" Sam asked Charlene. "It's really spooky."

"Once," Charlene said, "ages ago. But I wouldn't mind another look. I think I'll carry Tink, though. I need to save enough treats for the way back!"

Sam led the way through the dense

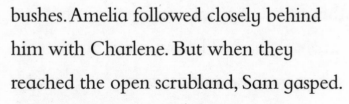

bushes. Amelia followed closely behind
him with Charlene. But when they
reached the open scrubland, Sam gasped.

"Look!" he said, pointing. Amelia's
heart lurched as she saw a black-and-
white bird flapping frantically on the
ground. She rushed towards it. She could
see some orange plastic netting tangled
around one of its wings. The bird had
flashes of red on its head and at the
base of its tail, and a long sharp beak.
It stopped flapping for a moment, and
Amelia could see its chest heaving for
breath. The bird's shiny black eyes looked
terrified and exhausted.

"Poor thing!" Charlene said.

"It's a greater spotted woodpecker," Amelia said, remembering a picture she'd seen in one of her gran's bird-watching books. "We have to help it!"

"But how?" Sam asked. "We don't have anything to cut it free, and it's a long walk to Animal Ark."

"I've got my phone," Charlene said. "Sam – hold Tink for a sec. I'll call the vet now."

While Charlene called, anger and sadness welled in Amelia's chest. She looked around the wilderness in despair.

If this place doesn't get cleaned up, this kind of thing is going to keep happening!

"Mr and Mrs Hope are on their way," Charlene said, as she hung up. "They said not to touch the bird, because it might get more stressed. I don't think having Tink nearby is helping, either. I'll take her back to the road. I can lead the Hopes here when they arrive."

"Good idea," Sam said, passing Tinkerbell back to Charlene. "We'll keep an eye on the woodpecker."

It felt like a long wait, watching the bird struggle and not being able to help it. But in less than ten minutes Charlene returned with the Hopes.

The woodpecker let out harsh warning calls as the vets approached it. But as soon as Mr Hope got a firm grip around its trembling body, the bird quietened down. Mrs Hope knelt before her husband, and with a small pair of scissors, carefully cut through the netting.

Amelia let out a breath of relief when Mrs Hope finally cut the last strand. Mr

Hope spread the wing that had been trapped, inspecting it.

"There's some damage to the wing base, so we'll have to take it in," he said. "But thanks to you three, it's only superficial. Left any longer it could have been much worse. You saved this little guy's life."

Amelia still felt cross. "It shouldn't have got hurt in the first place!" she said. "The next animal to get trapped or poisoned

here might not survive." Looking about at the discarded cans and plastic bags, Amelia realised she had to do something. "I'm coming back tomorrow," she said, "and I'm going to clean this mess up!"

"Count me in!" Sam said.

"Me too," Charlene added, scratching Tink behind the ears as she cradled her close.

"I think that's a great idea," Mr Hope said. "We certainly don't want any more

injuries like this!"

Mrs Hope held a wire cage steady for her husband, and he gently lifted the woodpecker in.

When the Hopes had headed back to their car, Charlene put Tinkerbell down on the ground. "Come on, Tink!" she said, taking a step and pulling the lead for the cat to follow.

Tink planted her paws, arched her back and hissed. Amelia crouched and held out a treat, but Tink sat down on her haunches and looked away, fur bristling.

Charlene tried pulling the lead again, but Tink hissed and spat, sinking her claws into the ground. "Oh, Tink! I'm not going to drag you!" Charlene picked the grumpy kitten up and stroked her fur back into place. "But if we can't walk you, and you don't like staying inside, I don't know how we're going to keep you happy!"

CHAPTER SIX

"Mum, can I borrow your gardening gloves?" Amelia asked, pulling a wodge of paper sacks out from the cupboard under the sink. "I'm going to meet Sam and Charlene at the wilderness today. We're going to clear it up so no other animals can get hurt by the rubbish."

"That's a great idea," her mum said, "but you won't have long. Your dad's picking you up in a couple of hours. You're going to his house this weekend, remember?"

Amelia froze, a sinking feeling in her stomach. She'd completely forgotten it was her weekend to visit her dad in York. "But I promised to meet the others, and we can't leave all that litter lying about!"

"Well, speak to your dad," her mum suggested. "Explain the problem. I'm sure you'll be able to work something out."

As Amelia dialled her dad's number, she felt torn. She wanted to spend time with her dad and didn't want to hurt his

feelings. But she was also really worried about the wilderness. *There are lives at stake!* By the time her dad answered, she almost couldn't bring herself to speak. But, when she explained the problem, her dad understood.

"It sounds like a really important project," Dad said. "So important that I'd like to help. Why don't I come and visit you this weekend, for a change? I could stay at Sam's parents' B&B that I've heard so much about."

"Really?" Amelia said, relief and excitement swelling inside her. "That would be awesome! You'll love the Old Mill – the breakfasts there are amazing!"

Amelia quickly explained where to go.

"I'll meet you there as soon as I can!" her dad promised.

After they had said their goodbyes, Amelia filled a bag with supplies, kissed her mum and her gran, and headed out to meet Sam and Charlene.

I don't care how long this takes, Amelia told herself. *I'm not stopping until the wilderness is safe!*

They had almost reached the wilderness when the sound of chatter and laughter rang out ahead. Amelia and Sam exchanged puzzled frowns, but Charlene grinned.

"I told some of my friends about what

happened to the woodpecker and they wanted to help too. It sounds like they beat us here," she explained.

"That's brilliant!" Amelia said.

"We might even finish today!" Sam added.

They pushed through the bushes into the wilderness and were met by a tall boy with his hair pulled back in a topknot.

"Hi, Christian!" Charlene said. "This is Amelia, and this is Sam."

"Hiya," the boy said.

"So, you're the masterminds behind the clean-up! We only arrived about half an hour ago, but we've got a bit of a system going." He pointed towards the undergrowth, where some of Charlene's classmates were shoving rubbish into sacks. "Green bags for paper and cans," Christian explained, "white bags for plastic, and black bags for anything else.

That way we can recycle as much as possible."

"Brilliant," Amelia said. "I brought paper sacks for anything compostable. This shouldn't take long at all!"

The sun shone brightly and a fresh, cool breeze made it perfect weather for working outside. Amelia quickly got stuck in, filling sacks with rubbish. She

couldn't help puzzling over some of the items she found – a battery from an old phone, a bundle of clothes hangers, even a cracked leather shoe. Christian found a broken cassette player that had probably

been there since before the train station closed.

"Hello!" Amelia's dad called, as he arrived towards the end of the morning. "You all look like you're doing a great job!"

After Amelia had

introduced him to everyone, he set to work loading the rubbish bags into the boot of his car to take to the recycling centre.

By lunchtime, almost all the rubbish was gone. Charlene had even brought a spray bottle and cloth, to scrub the sign near the signal box. As Amelia collected the last bits of litter from around the building, she heard a sudden *ratatatat* coming from high in one of the trees.

"That's a woodpecker!" she cried. She spotted a flash of red in the branches and

pointed. "Look, up there!"

Charlene shaded her eyes. "I see it!"
she said. "I wonder if it's the mate of
the bird we rescued." She looked about
the wilderness and smiled. "Now all
the rubbish has gone, this place will be
a perfect habitat for wildlife. When the
Hopes bring the other woodpecker back,
maybe they'll even lay eggs!"

Amelia felt a surge of excitement as an
idea popped into her head. "This area
was dangerous for wildlife, but we've
made it safe by clearing it up," she said.
"Well, what if we could make a safe
outdoor space for Tink?"

Charlene raised her eyebrow. "What do

you mean?" she asked, puzzled.

Amelia thought of the rectangle of lawn behind the Girtzes' house, enclosed by high fences. "How about we make your garden a safe habitat for a deaf kitten?" she explained, grinning.

"It's worth a try," said Charlene.

And it might just work! thought Amelia.

CHAPTER SEVEN

Back in Charlene's living room, Amelia
could barely stay still as she waited with
Sam and her dad, listening to Charlene
explain the plan to her parents. From the
Girtzes' nods and smiles she could tell
they liked the idea.

"We can put chicken wire around the

top of the fence, and a cat flap in the garden gate that only lets the other cats through," Charlene finished, her face flushed with excitement.

"You know, I think one more day trapped in the house is going to drive Tink barmy," Mr Girtz said. "Not to mention all the things she'll destroy … or poop on. Let's do it!"

Mrs Girtz nodded, smiling. "I'll go to the garden centre to pick up some wire and another cat flap," she said. "Maybe while I'm gone you can make the garden more like a playground for her?"

Amelia's mind started to race. As soon as Mrs Girtz had left, they all went through to the conservatory. The garden was just a patch of lawn with beds around the edge and a few pot plants.

"I've seen a video of cats using a drying rack as a climbing frame," Amelia said. "Can I put that one outside?" She pointed to the wooden rack standing in the conservatory.

"We can do better than that!" Mr Girtz said. "I'll make a proper climbing frame for Tink so she can scratch as much as

she likes. I've got spare wood and logs somewhere." He turned to Amelia's dad. "Do you mind lending a hand?"

"Not at all – in fact, I was just going to volunteer," Amelia's dad said.

"And I'll make a den for Tink to hide in!" Charlene chimed in.

Before long, the Girtzes' conservatory had been transformed into a busy workshop. In one corner, Charlene was weaving bendy willow sticks together to make a den. Mr Girtz and Amelia's dad set to work with logs and planks of wood, making a kitten jungle-gym that looked a bit like a gnarled old tree. Amelia and Sam tied bright scraps of

96

fabric to the branches, like leaves.

Eventually, they were ready to move
everything into the garden. Sam pushed
the pot plants together to create a shady
hunting ground. Mr Girtz installed the
scratching tree, complete with branches

and a platform to sit on, right in the
centre of the garden.

Amelia found an old plastic washing-
up bowl in the kitchen. She filled it with
water and put some of the kitten's hollow
plastic balls inside, so they would bob
around. "Now Tink can pretend to fish!"
she told Sam, setting it down near the
plant pots.

Finally, Charlene brought out her
wicker cat den. The upside-down
basket made a small igloo-like den,
and Charlene put a waterproof cushion
inside to make it cosy. Then she fetched a
selection of cat toys. "Let's hide these
all around the garden for Tink to

discover," she said.

Once they had finished, Amelia looked around the transformed space and smiled. "She'll love it!"

"I can't wait to let her out!" Charlene said. Then, at the sound of a car pulling up, Charlene's eyes went wide. "That will be Mum!" Before long, Mrs Girtz came into the garden carrying a huge roll of chicken wire.

"You've been busy!" she said, admiring the new installations. "It looks great! The next bit's going to be down to us adults,

though. Why don't you kids go inside
and keep Tink busy while we put this on
the fence? And Charlene – maybe make
some sandwiches? I'll bet your friends are
starving!"

As Charlene went into the kitchen to
make lunch, Sam and Amelia found Tink
ripping curls of wicker from the leg of a
chair in the conservatory. Amelia picked
up a leftover strip of fabric, then stamped.

Tink looked up and Amelia pulled the fabric along the floor, making it wiggle. Tink watched it, her eyes wide and her tail twitching. She pounced on the fabric and started to gnaw at it.

Sam picked up another piece of fabric and tied it to the end of a wicker cane. "We should be able to keep her busy for a while with all these leftovers," he said.

"Not long now, Tink," said Amelia.

"You'll soon have your very own outdoor playground!"

Once the children had finished eating their sandwiches, Mr Girtz rapped on the conservatory window. Amelia looked out to see an arc of wire all along the top of the fence, curving sharply inwards so Tink couldn't climb it and escape.

"It's ready!" Charlene cried, leaping to her feet. She opened the conservatory door. Tink looked up, her nose twitching as she sniffed the air from outside. She rushed towards the open door, stopping on the threshold to peer out.

Go on, Tink! Amelia thought.

A sudden breeze made the strips of

102

fabric on the makeshift tree flutter and dance. Tink bristled all over, the wind stirring her fur, then streaked across the garden and straight up the trunk. Amelia grinned as the tiny kitten sprang on to a branch, then tumbled over it to hang upside down. Instead of righting herself, Tink batted at the fabric leaves, clinging on with her other three paws. With her ears flat against her head and her blue eyes darting about, she looked ready for anything.

Amelia giggled.

"I'd say that's a win!" Mr Girtz said, smiling.

Charlene rushed over to her parents,

wrapping them both in a hug. "Thank you!" she said. Then she turned to where Amelia stood with her dad and Sam. "Thank you, too! I was so worried Tink would never be happy, but this has been the best day ever!"

Amelia and Sam exchanged a grin. As her dad squeezed her hand and smiled at her with pride, Amelia had to agree.

CHAPTER EIGHT

"Out you get, then!" Amelia's dad said as he pulled up in the layby near the wilderness, two weeks later.

Amelia, Sam and Charlene all piled out, then hefted bags and tools from the boot. They had met at the Girtzes' house after school every day for the past two weeks. Together they had made nesting boxes for birds and cut holes in tennis balls to make tiny nests for dormice. By filling wooden frames with hollow bamboo sticks and old pinecones they had even made several bug hotels. Sam hadn't been sure about those, but Amelia had promised there wouldn't be any tarantulas coming to visit – like when the arachnologist Dr Rutland had come to stay at the B&B!

Mr Hope had called Amelia the night before and told her they would be releasing the woodpecker the next day. With only a few hours to go before the bird's release, they still had lots to do so Amelia's dad had come back to help again. Amelia couldn't wait to put everything into place.

Her dad set to work with shears, cutting back brambles while Sam and Amelia pulled up weeds. Charlene nailed hand-painted signs to the trunk of an old

Woodpeckers
roosting
Do not disturb

tree and to the signal-box door. Amelia's dad mounted the bird boxes to trees while Amelia held the base of his ladder. Insects buzzed around them as they

worked, and birds sang in the treetops. Even though it had only been two weeks, Amelia noticed that there seemed to be more wildlife. While Sam fixed the dormouse nests to the trunks of saplings, Charlene hid the bug hotels deep inside shady bushes.

By the time they had finished, Amelia felt hot and tired. Itchy bramble scratches covered her arms and she had blisters on her hands from all the woodwork she'd done after school. But, standing with her friends and looking over the wildlife refuge they had created, she let out a contented sigh.

"We'll have to give this place a proper

110

name now," she said.

They had only just managed to load
their tools back into the car boot when
the Hopes pulled up in their van. Mr
Hope took a cage covered with a blanket
from the back, and Mrs Hope put a
finger to her lips. "Everyone stay quiet, so
we don't frighten the woodpecker," she
whispered.

They made the short walk to the

wilderness in silence. When they arrived,
Mr Hope set the woodpecker's cage on
an old tree stump. As he removed the
blanket, Amelia caught sight of the bird
inside, its wings neatly folded.

"Stay well back," Mrs Hope whispered,
as her husband opened the cage door.

The bird stood
still for a long
moment, its
head cocked as
if listening. Then,
without warning,
it spread its wings
and fluttered
away. Amelia felt

a strange pang of
longing and joy
as she watched it
swoop through the
trees and quickly
vanish from sight.

"That couldn't have gone better," Mr
Hope said. "Good job, everyone."

"Yes, and well done for all the work
you've done here," Mrs Hope said. "As
long as someone checks the area over
every now and again for rubbish, I'm
sure we won't have to rescue any more
animals."

"Listen!" Amelia's dad said suddenly.
A slow grin spread over his face and his

head tipped to one side.

RATATATATAT!

The noise was coming from the treetops high above them. *A woodpecker!* Amelia quickly realised. *No … not* one *woodpecker … two!*

"There!" Charlene said, pointing towards the top of the oak tree to which she'd nailed her sign. Amelia peered up and saw the two birds tapping away, one on either side of the trunk.

"I'm guessing there might be even more woodpeckers here before long!" Mr Hope said. "And all thanks to your hard work!"

Once the Hopes had left, Charlene, Sam and Amelia followed Amelia's dad back to the car.

"Why don't you stop by our house on the way back?" Charlene asked. "Dad's made some home-made lemonade, and you can see how Tink's getting on."

"Sounds good to me!" Amelia's dad said, starting the car.

Before long they pulled up at the Girtzes' house. Charlene led them straight through to the garden, where

Amelia grinned to see all three kittens clambering around the climbing frame tree, tumbling over each other and swiping at leaves.

Tiger Lily stood by Amelia's pretend fish pond. The big cat dabbed daintily at a floating ball. As it bobbed away, Tiger Lily snatched her paw back, shook it dry, then stalked away, her nose in the air.

"Tiger Lily still isn't sure about the water feature," Charlene said, "but now that the garden's so

much fun, none of the cats want to leave. Tink's hardly ever alone any more."

Charlene's mum soon came out with a tray of glasses. Amelia, Sam and Charlene sat on the lawn with Amelia's dad, watching the kittens play and drinking the sharp, sweet lemonade.

"Watch this," Charlene said, setting down her glass. She held her hand out towards the climbing tree with her fingers pinched together as if she were holding out a treat for her kitten. Tink instantly leapt down and trotted over to her.

"That's awesome!" Sam said. "I thought it would take way longer

to train her than that, after our first attempt."

"That was because she was so fed up," Charlene said. "Now that she's happy, she's picking up hand signals really quickly." Charlene leaned over her kitten and started to purr. Tink nudged her pink nose up against Charlene's cheek, and

 started to purr right back.

"Oh my goodness!" Amelia said. "That's too cute!"

Suddenly the bright lights in the conservatory flashed

on and off. All at once, the four cats raced across the lawn, scrambling over each other to go into the house.

"What's going on?" Amelia's dad asked.

Charlene giggled. "That's the signal for dinner."

Amelia watched through the glass door as Mrs Girtz set four bowls on the floor, one big one and three small ones. Tiger Lily got stuck straight into her dinner, while the three kittens raced to the smaller bowls. Once Smee had finished gobbling up his food, he crossed to Tink's bowl, and shoved her aside. Tink let out a squeak so loud Amelia could hear her from the garden. Then the little white

kitten batted Smee on the head with her paw, pushed him away with her head, and carried on eating her dinner.

Amelia, Sam and Charlene all laughed. Even Amelia's dad chuckled. Amelia turned to wrap him in a big, gleeful hug. "Thank you for helping us, Dad," she said. "I think it's safe to say Tink's going to be just fine!"

The End

Turn over for a sneak peek at
Amelia and Sam's next adventure!

ANiMAL ARK

Llama on the Loose

Lucy Daniels

"Look, Sam, I can see Lliam! Or is that Llarry?" Amelia Haywood peered through the car window at a pair of long white llama ears sticking up behind the hedge. She had been best friends with Sam since she had moved to Welford and they had started helping out at Animal Ark, the local veterinary surgery. This morning they were travelling with the vets, Mr and Mrs Hope, to check up on the animals at the Parish family's petting farm before school.

"It's probably Lliam," said Sam, leaning over her shoulder. "He likes that corner of the field."

As they drew closer to the petting farm,

Amelia heard the bleating of goats and clucking of chickens and she broke into a wide smile.

"How do you know it's not the new llama?" Mr Hope asked from the front passenger seat. He turned to peer at Amelia and Sam over his glasses.

"Caleb said Llucinda's brown," Sam explained. Their friend Caleb had been talking all week about the new llama his family had adopted.

"I can't wait to meet her!" sighed Amelia as excitement swelled in her chest.

Mrs Hope smiled at Amelia through the rear-view mirror, her green eyes twinkling, as she pulled into the farmhouse driveway.

The Hopes really understand why I love animals … because they love them too!

Caleb leapt off the farmhouse porch as Amelia got out of the car. He jogged down the gravel pathway towards them. "Come and see Llucinda! She's so cute!"

Amelia glanced back at the Hopes, who were rummaging in the boot of their car. She and Sam had come along to help them, really.

Mr Hope lifted out his black case, full of medicines and paperwork. "You two go on and meet the new llama," he said. "The goats won't take long, and we can manage the chickens and pigs quite easily. We'll save the llamas for last!"

Amelia grinned at Sam, and they both broke into a run, following Caleb up the drive. He led them down the side of the house and through the petting farm.

**Read Llama on the Loose
to find out what happens next ...**

Animal Advice

Do you love animals as much as Amelia and Sam? Here are some tips on how to look after them from veterinary surgeon Sarah McGurk.

Caring for your pet

1. Animals need clean water at all times.

2. They need to be fed too – ask your vet what kind of food is best, and how much the animal needs.

3. Some animals, such as dogs, need exercise every day.

4. Animals also need lots of love. You should always be very gentle with your pets and be careful not to do anything that might hurt them.

When to go to the vet

Sometimes animals get ill. Like you, they will mostly get better on their own. But if your pet has hurt itself or seems very unwell, then a trip to the vet might be needed. Some pets also need to be vaccinated, to prevent them from getting dangerous diseases. Your vet can tell you what your pet needs.

Helping wildlife

1 Always ask an adult before you go near any animals you don't know.

2 If you find an animal or bird which is injured or can't move, it is best not to touch it.

3 If you are worried, you can phone an animal charity such as the RSPCA (SSPCA in Scotland) for help.

Where animals need you!

Kitten Rescue
Lucy Daniels

Bunny Trouble
Lucy Daniels

Fox Cub Danger
Lucy Daniels

Puppy in Peril
Lucy Daniels

The Purrfect Sleepover
Lucy Daniels

Doggy Drama
Lucy Daniels

Runaway Hamster
Lucy Daniels

Guinea Pig Superstar
Lucy Daniels

The Lonely Pony
Lucy Daniels

Scaredy-Dog
Lucy Daniels

Lost Kitten
Lucy Daniels

Llama on the Loose
Lucy Daniels

www.animalark.co.uk